THIS IS ONE OF ONE THOUSAND COPIES

JONATHAN CARROLL

DAVE MCKEAN

THE HEIDELBERG CYLINDER

JONATHAN CARROLL

Also by
Jonathan Carroll

The Wooden Sea (2001)
The Marriage of Sticks
Kissing the Beehive
The Panic Hand
After Silence
From the Teeth of Angels
Black Cocktail
Outside the Dog Museum
Sleeping In Flame
A Child Across the Sky
Bones of the Moon
Voice of Our Shadow
The Land of Laughs

www.jonathancarroll.com

This is a work of fiction. Names, characters, places,
And incidents either are the product of the author's
imagination or are used fictitiously. Any resemblance
to actual events, locales, organizations, or persons,
living or dead, is entirely coincidental and beyond
the intent of either the author or the publisher.

MOBIUS NEW MEDIA
2205 Silverside Road, Suite #5
Wilmington, Delaware 19810

Cover art by Dave McKean
Book design and layout by Joe del Tufo
ISBN: 0-9703786-0-2

First Mobius New Media Printing: October 2000
Printed in the U.S.A.

FIRST EDITION

www.mobiusnm.com

For Joe del Tufo--
in friendship and thanks

THE HEIDELBERG CYLINDER

THE HEIDELBERG CYLINDER

It began the day our new refrigerator was delivered. A big silver thing that looked like a miniature Airstream trailer turned on its side. But Rae loved it. We had bought it a few days before. In January I told her as soon as my raise comes in, you get your fridge. And I kept my promise, all six hundred and thirty-nine dollars of it.

Two puffing deliverymen came in the pouring rain to curse and shove it into place in our kitchen. Both guys were in big bad moods, that was plain. But no wonder-- who wants to deliver appliances in a ripping thunderstorm? When they were finished and I'd signed the delivery papers, Rae offered coffee. That perked them up. After they'd done stirring and sipping and settling into the chairs one guy, "Dennis" it said on his shirt, told a strange story that got us thinking.

For the past few days while driving around making deliveries, they'd seen piles of furniture all over town stacked in the middle of sidewalks. That didn't seem so strange to me. But Dennis said they saw it at least ten times overall: Big piles of furniture heaped up, just sitting there unguarded usually.

"No that's not true," his partner Vito piped in. "Remember when we saw the man and woman standing next to a pile up on Lail Avenue, arguing? They were really fighting! Arms flying, pointing fingers at each other... It was like one had thrown the other outta the house with all their stuff, but you couldn't tell who'd thrown who."

"Just furniture? Nothing else? No moving vans there or anything? No people guarding the stuff?"

"Nope, that's the weird part. These piles of furniture and boxes, like whole households, stacked up and no one around. Go figure."

The four of us sat there drinking coffee, thinking it over. Then Dennis said, "We saw another pile coming over here today. Remember that nice blue leather couch and TV I pointed to? Jeez, stuff looked brand new. Big screen TV... Just sitting out in the rain getting drenched.

"Times are tough. Maybe it's coincidence, but I hear a lotta people are being thrown out of their houses by the banks."

"All at the same time? I don't think so, partner." Vito said sarcastically to him and winked at me.

Dennis straightened up and threw him a black look. "You got a better explanation, genius?"

"Nope. Just that it's weird. Never in my life have I seen stuff that nice left out alone on the street unguarded. And so many times. In the rain? Makes the whole town look like a big yard sale."

Right then Chapter Two began but none of us knew it yet. Before anyone had a chance to say more, the doorbell rang. I looked at Rae to see if she was expecting someone. She shook her head. Who now?

I got up to answer it. A second after opening that door I wished I hadn't. Standing on my porch were two guys looking like wet seals. One glimpse and you wanted to say, "No thanks to whatever you've got," slam the door in their faces and run for cover.

Naturally they were smiling. But you know the kind-- totally fake. No one smiles like that without putting too much face into it. Or they got a gun stuck in their back. These guys were wearing identical brown suits freckled dark all over with rain. Bright yellow plastic nametags were pinned on their breast pockets. White shirts with the top button buttoned but no ties. Both had bowl haircuts that made them look like monks or The Beatles gone bad. And they smelled. I'm sorry to have to say that, but they did. They smelled like they'd lived in their buttoned- up rayon shirts way way too long.

"Good morning Sir! I'm Brother Brooks and this is Brother Zin Zan."

"Brother who? You want to say all that again?" I stood back and gave them a lot of room, just in case they exploded and their crazy went all over my porch.

"Brooks and Zin Zan. Would you have a few moments to spare? It may just change your life!"

I knew where this was leading and was just about to adios them, but a thunderclap shook the house and rain came down like a tidal wave. What could I do, shove them back out in that flood? Really unhappily I asked, "You want to come in a minute?"

Their faces lit up like Yankee Stadium for a night game. "We certainly would! Thank you very much."

In for a penny, in for a pound. "Want some coffee? Looks like you could use it."

"No thank you, sir. But it's certainly kind of you to offer."

"Well, come on in." They stepped into the hall and I closed the door. They both wore black basketball sneakers with a brand name written in white on the side that I couldn't make out. I thought it was kind of strange that Bible guys would be wearing sneakers. Much less underneath a suit.

"Bill, who was it?" Rae called out.

"Brooks Brothers and Sen Sen." I couldn't resist saying. And you know what? Brooks started laughing.

"That's very funny, sir. People always make that mistake. But actually, it's Brother Brooks. And Brother Zin Zan. He's from New Zealand."

"New Zealand. Is that right? You're pretty far from home. Sorry for the mistake. Come on in."

I went first to see what would happen. When Rae and the delivery guys caught a view of who was following me, they got exactly the same look on their faces-- Whaaat?

"Everybody, this is Brother Brooks and Brother Zin Zan. They say they can change our lives." I said it like I was introducing an act in Las Vegas.

Picking right up on it Dennis said, "That sounds good to me. Anything to stop delivering refrigerators!"

Rae stared at me like I'd gone nuts. Both of us hate door to door preachers with their ridiculous religions and too many teeth. Her face asked why had I let these guys in? Suddenly our house was like the dog pound-- every stray in town under one roof, dripping on her carpets.

I sat down but the Brothers kept standing. To my surprise, Zin Zan started talking. He had a strong accent. Then I remembered he was from New Zealand. The whole time he spoke, Brooks gave him an all-attention smile that looked as phony as a tinfoil Christmas tree.

"We represent a brotherhood called The Heidelberg Cylinder. Our avatar is a man named Beeflow."

"Beef-low?" Dennis looked at his partner and me, then wiggled his eyebrows and O'd his mouth.

"No sir, Bee-flow. We believe we are entering the Second Diaspora. It will formally begin with the Millennium and continue for another 16,312 years."

"Sixteen thousand, you say? With or without intermissions?"

My sweet wife tried to smooth that one over. "Would you two like some juice?"

"Thank you, Ma'am, but we don't drink anything but water. Beeflow says-"

"Who's this Beeflow?"

"Our spiritual master. Chosen avatar by--"

"What's an avatar? Sounds like that new model Honda."

Brother Brooks liked that one too. He smiled and for the first time it looked like a real smile. "No sir, an avatar is an incarnation of a deity. A kind of God in human form, you could say."

"What did your Mr. Beeflow do before he became God?"

Maybe it was the way Rae said it, so respectful and serious. Or maybe because Dennis and I were watching each other when she spoke. Whatever, as soon as my wife asked her question so gently, the three of us guys cracked up. I mean big time. We laughed so hard we choked.

"He was a travel agent."

"Good career move!" I said, which brought down the house again. Except for Rae. She Fed-Ex'd me her stone face and I knew what <u>that</u> meant. I shut up fast.

"So what do you guys believe in? I mean, like a quick wrap-up of your religion?"

"We believe in rent control, a river view when possible, and forced air heating."

The living room got silent fast. Real silent.

"Say that again?"

"Room, sir. We believe in the just and proper distribution of room. Human space. Apartments, houses, it makes no difference. A civilized place to live."

"Geodesic domes." Zin Zan added, nodding.

"What the <u>hell</u> are you talking about? I'm not following you here, Brother Brooks."

"Well sir, have you noticed all of the furniture out on the streets of the town recently? Piles of it, looking like it's waiting to be picked up?"

"We were just talking about that!"

"It is the first sign of the beginning of the Diaspora."

"What's that?"

"A Diaspora is the breaking up and scattering of a people. The forced re-settling of people far from their ancestral homelands."

"You mean they're being moved out?"

"Yes, exactly."

"By who? Who's moving them?"

"Satan."

I cleared my throat and snatched a quick glimpse of Rae. She gave me a look that said, "Don't make trouble with these guys." So instead of cracking wise about the Satanic Moving Company, I looked at the others to see if they were going to snap at the bait.

"All those piles of stuff out on the streets are there because the Devil's throwing people out of their houses? Why's he doin' that?"

Zin Zan picked it up. "Because Hell is filled to overflowing Sir, and Satan needs the room. He plans to re-populate the earth with the fallen."

I didn't know about the others but I was so embarrassed by the direction this conversation was taking that I could only stare at the floor and hope those Brothers would evaporate by the time I looked up again.

"So you're saying that if I'm bad and die now, there's no room for me in Hell and I may end up back here, living next door?" Vito said in a voice full of "you gotta be shittin' me."

My eyes still down, I heard Zin Zan's thick accent field the question. "Why do you think the world's in such bad straits, Sir? New fatal diseases being discovered every day, crime the likes of which defy human imagination. How do you explain people's vast and unfailing indifference to one another?

"Because so many of them are dead. They have no souls. This has been going on for some time. The dead bring death back with them when they return to earth."

What can you say to something as looney-tuney as that? I felt like taking a nap. I felt like getting up from where I was sitting, maybe or maybe not giving a wave to everyone in the room, and walking right out of there into the bedroom and my pillow and about an hour of nighty-night. My brain felt tired and like it had had something lousy and too heavy for breakfast.

"Yeah? Well prove it, Brothers." Dennis spoke like he was spitting and said that last word like a black soul brother. You know, he said it 'bruddas' and there wasn't any respect in the word.

Not that it touched the Heidelberg Cylinder boys. They smiled on like two "Ken" dolls on a date with Barbie. Brooks politely asked, "What do you mean, sir?"

Dennis pointed a 'it's your fault' finger at him and shook it. "You know exactly what I mean. Guys like you have been coming to my door for years, talking about how the world's gonna end tomorrow. God's gonna kick my butt for sinning unless I repent. Armageddon's coming so watch out! Well you know what? Arma-geddon pretty damned sick of hearing that stuff from your like. If you think you're so right about what you're saying, prove it. That's all-- show us it's true. You say the Devil's on earth moving dead people out of their houses? Show me!"

Vito put a thumbs up. "I agree! Show me too!"

I kind of felt like doing it too. I myself was sick of gleamy-eyed wackos coming to my house with their cheap pamphlets and 'God's-gonna-get-you' threats. Having the big fat nerve to tell me I'd done everything wrong with my life. And I'd better start dancing to their tune or else. Oh yeah? How do you know; you been watching my every move?

What I resented most was how damned sure people like this were that they were right. Hey, maybe they were, but how could they be so convinced? I admit I wasn't sure of anything in life, much less how His Majesty upstairs in heaven makes things work. But at least I admit it. Listening to these duds talk, or others like them who'd appeared over the years with their own smudged magazines and weird smiles, God was as easy to understand as the baseball scores.

"Well?"

The not-so Righteous Brothers blinked at the same time and smiled again. But kept their traps shut.

"Huh? Can you prove you're right? Or are you going to tell me to wait till Judgement Day rolls around to find out?"

"Oh no sir, we can show you right now. That's not a problem." Brooks spoke and his voice was as nice as rice. I mean he spoke like what Dennis had just asked was the easiest favor in the world to grant. You want me to show you Satan? You want me to open up the back of the big clock and show you how it ticks? Follow me, sir-- This way to Satan. Just like that. Simple.

"What the <u>fuck</u> are you guys talking about?"

Rae caught her breath hearing my word, but I couldn't help myself. I was suddenly as hot and sizzling as a frying chicken. I didn't like where this conversation was going. And I sure didn't believe what was just said. All eyes were on me like the kid who just farted in class. Dennis and Vito's faces said ha ha, but Rae's was uh oh because she knows my temper. The Brothers were calm as usual.

"You can sit there with a straight face and say you'll show me Satan this minute?"

"We can show you proof, sir. All the proof you'll need. We just have to go up to Pilot Hill."

"What's on Pilot Hill?"

"The proof you want."

"What proof?"

The brothers stood up. "We can go right now. We'll give you a thousand dollars each if you're not happy with our proof."

The room went stone quiet for the second time in ten minutes.

Rae said in a wiggly voice,"A thousand dollars?"

"Oh yes, Ma'am. We have no desire to waste your valuable time." Brooks reached into his pocket and pulled out a roll of bills as thick as a Big Mac. So help me God, that man's hands contained more cash than I'd ever seen one person hold, outside of a bank teller.

Vito whistled one note low and asked what I'm sure we were all wondering: "How much you got there?"

Brooks looked at his hand. "I think ten thousand dollars. How much do you have, Brother Zin Zan?"

Zin stuck out his lower lip and nodded. "Ten thousand." He patted his pocket.

"Each of you guys is carrying ten grand?" Dennis's amazed voice cracked halfway through the sentence.

"That's the way we do things in our organization, sir. We want you to be happy with your decision, one way or the other."

Vito stood right up. "Well I just made my decision—let's go!"

Dennis too. "I'm with you. Pilot Hill, here we come."

Rae looked at me and then stood up slowly. The Brothers did too. Only I stayed where I was sitting. To emphasize that fact even more I crossed my arms and went humph.

"What's the matter, Bill?"

"You know damned well what the matter is, Rae! This whole thing is nuts. The three of you are going out the door with these screw-balls because they dangled some free money in front of you. Dangled but didn't give. Well how about this—I'll come too if you give me my thousand dollars right now, Brothers. Not later—this second. I'll give it back to you when we get there if I'm so convinced you're right."

"I'm fine with that, Sir. It's no problem," Brooks said and without one second's hesitation peeled ten crisp new hundred-dollar bills off his Big Mac. "Here you go." He crossed the room and handed them to me.

"Hey, I want mine too if he's getting his now!"

"Me too."

"Yes, me too please." Rae said that. She is a shy kind woman who doesn't even complain when someone big steps on her toe at the market. But now here she was wanting her thousand dollars up front just like everyone else. I was setting a bad example, but at least we were all a thousand dollars richer for it.

Then an evil thought came riding in. I looked suspiciously at the money in my hand. Maybe it was too fresh, too new? Was real money really that green? "How do we know this isn't fake? That it's not counterfeit or something?"

Brother Zin Zan was counting off hundreds while Brooks was handing Vito his share. "Oh we can stop at a bank on the way and have it checked if you like. But I guarantee you it's real."

I looked at my money like it might have something to say. This whole thing was so crazy, why shouldn't we just accept it at face value? Four thousand dollars was being handed out in that room and everyone was as cool as cucumbers about it. Like it happened to us every day and now was just the payoff hour. Rae wore a smile that was somewhere between happiness and crime.

"How do you want to go over there?"

"What do you mean?"

Dennis waved his hand around the room. "Well there's six of us. You want us all to go in your car?"

Zin Zan shook his head. "We don't have a car."

I shook mine. "We got a little Hyundai. We can barely get the two of us into it. It wouldn't know what to do with six people."

"It'd have a heart attack." Rae said and it was like the first joke she'd made in five years.

All the guys smiled at her and I felt pretty proud to have a wisecracking wife. First she's putting out a greedy hand just like the others for a thousand dollars and now she was cracking jokes. She was suddenly a completely different woman from the one I knew but I kind of liked it.

"Then I say we all go in the truck."

"What truck, yours? And ride in the back with the rest of the appliances?"

"Naah-- You and your wife can sit up front with Dennis. Me and the Brothers will get in back."

Brooks and Zin Zan nodded to that and so did Rae. Who was I to argue? We put on our raincoats and waded out into the storm. Where I looked left and right but didn't see any furniture truck. "So where is it?"

"Right there. Right in front of you."

Right in front of me was a red truck. But on the side of it was a picture of a smiling white pig wearing a black baseball cap. The poor little guy was being roasted on a spit. Now I ask you, why would you put a baseball cap on a pig you were cooking? Even more, why would the pig be smiling while it died? Above that dumbass picture was written "Lester's Meat." Which when you thought about it didn't sound very appetizing either. I made myself a mental note never to buy Lester's Meat.

"That's a meat truck."

"It's my uncle's. He lets me use it to make deliveries sometimes."

"You deliver appliances in a meat truck?"

"It's been known to happen." Vito and Dennis grinned at each other like they knew something we didn't.

"This is too weird. My new refrigerator was in there up alongside a side of beef?"

"No, the truck's empty now. He only lets me use it when it's empty."

"Yeah, but is my fridge going to smell of raw meat now?"

"I'm afraid we're going to have to walk," Brooks said.

"Walk? Why?"

"Because members of the Heidelberg Cylinder are strict vegetarians. Not vegan but strict vegetarian. We don't eat anything with a face. We avoid contact with any form of meat."

"What the Hell are you talking about? You're not having contact with meat. We're going to Pilot Hill, like you wanted."

"I'm sorry, but we're not allowed contact with anything to do with meat. If there's a remnant in that truck it could contaminate us. No, it's out of the question. Brother Zin Zan and I will walk up to Pilot Hill and meet you there."

"It's three miles away. It'll take you an hour to get there! Look, I got a better idea—you guys get in the front and we'll all get in the back. I don't mind being contaminated by meat. Rae?"

She nodded. The Brothers looked at each other and shrugged that the idea was okay with them. Which is how we ended up standing inside a cold empty truck holding on for dear life while getting real intimate with the smell of fresh beef and etcetera. Then about three minutes after the ride began, the only little light bulb back there that lit anything flickered-flickered-flickered and went out. Poof-- Total blackness.

"Real cozy back here, huh?" Vito said from somewhere nearby in the blackness.

"I can't see a damned thing."

"Not much to see. Just a bunch of empty space."

"Bill?" Rae's voice was small and like she was far away.

"Yeah?"

"I'm scared now. I don't think I want to go."

"Why's that? You were fast enough taking their money." I threw in with a little twist-of-the-knife in my voice.

"I know, but I gotta bad feeling now."

"Why?"

"Because those men are so sure of themselves. They got pockets full of money and can give away a thousand dollars just like that to prove they're right."

"Four thousand dollars."

Vito made his whistle again. "Four thousand smackers. Did you ever carry four thousand dollars in your pocket? From the way they talked, it sounds like these guys do it every day. Kind of tempting when you think about it, you know?"

The darkness felt like it was suddenly heavier. So did the silence that followed what he'd said.

"What's your point?"

Vito tried to sound light but I heard the rats gathering on the other side of his voice. "Well, there's twenty thousand dollars sitting up there next to the driver. That's a lot of money."

"Bill-"

A hand touched me on the elbow and I assumed it was Rae's. I patted it until I realized it was too damned big for her hand and that it was Vito's instead.

I gave him a fast hard poke that couldn't have felt good. "Just what the Hell are you doing?"

"Nothing, man. Take it easy. It's dark in here, in case you didn't notice. I'm just trying to get my bearings."

"Well, get them away from me."

Why was he touching my elbow in the dark like that? And why was he making suggestions like maybe we should do something criminal about the twenty thousand dollars sitting in the Brothers' pockets at that very minute?

"Bill?"

"What Rae?" I said it pretty harshly and angry voices are not that woman's favorite music. Sure enough, her answer came back at me like a flame-thrower.

"Don't you talk to me like that, Bill Gallatin! I don't like any of this. I want to go home. They can have their money back. I don't care. I just want to go back home now."

"Well honey, wait till we stop and they let us out. There's not much we can do till then."

"But we should be there by now. It's not that far. How come we haven't gotten there yet?"

I took a deep breath and licked my tongue back and forth across my lips which is usually my procedure when I'm trying hard to stay calm. When I was sure I had my temper back on its leash I spoke. "I don't know why we aren't there yet, sweetheart. Pilot Hill's on the other side of town, remember. It takes a little while to get there."

"I want to get out of this truck right now; it's creepy and weird."

"Well sure it is—it's pitch black and we're standing in the back of a meat truck!"

"I don't mean that."

"Well what do you mean, Rae?" I lost my composure and my voice came out sounding damned irritated.

The next thing I knew, my good wife's crying because she's scared, while at the same time I'm realizing this is all my fault basically. I was the one who invited Brother Brooks and Zin Zan into our house not one hour ago. Before them everything was just fine—we had a new refrigerator, we were shooting the breeze with the movers and finishing our coffee.

Before I had a chance to say anything more, the truck began slowing. Then it stopped with a jerk that sent us all flying, judging by the sound of things around me. Vito yelled "Hey!" and Rae squealed, but I was quiet because it was all I could do to stop from falling flat on my face. My mother used to say never try standing up when the bus is going around a corner. Now I had one to add to that--Never try keeping your balance in the dark. You need to see stuff so you can judge angles and tilts. At that moment I couldn't see anything so I was groping out with my hands, basically reaching for whatever would have me.

Unfortunately I found something.

What's warm and furry and licks your hand in the dark? A dark that had gotten ten times darker because all of a sudden it was totally silent in there except for the sound of me being slurpy-licked by an eager tongue.

"Shit!" I yanked my hand and body back like they'd been in fire and doing so, lost my balance after touching something warm and furry. I didn't know where I was falling because it was whoa-whoa-whoa backward. But still it was away from the tongue and that was all that mattered.

I fell on my ass. One of those breath-death drops where you land Bullseye on the tenderest part of your spine. It sent an atomic jolt of pain up to the tips of my ears and then shivered back down my body, gradually looking for a place to stop.

When I could breathe again around the pain, I said "Rae?" Nothing. Then I said "Vito?" Silence. Nothing but me, the dark and whatever thing had licked me.

"Mr. Gallatin? My name is Beeflow. I'll be your guide now."

The voice was right next to my ear. Right next to it. I was on my ass, remember. It was a nice voice-- smooth and low-- but without warning hearing it so close to me in that all-out darkness… Know what my first thought was? The very first one?

Is it little?

Is this thing standing up, or bending down to talk into my ear? How big is it? Not what is it, or how did it suddenly get two inches from my ear.

How big is it.

Then I tried sliding away from whatever it was.

"Don't be afraid."

"Get away from me! Where are the others? Rae?"

"You needn't worry; they're fine."

"Prove they're fine."

"Bill, we're fine."

"Rae?"

"Yes sweetie, don't worry. I'm in Los Angeles."

"What? Where? What?"

"Yes! I'm at the Universal Studio tour with Vito. We're about to go into the 'Back to the Future' ride. I'm so excited!"

Her voice sounded like she was talking on a telephone. In her background was a lot of noise-- kids shouting and laughter, some sounds I didn't recognize. Then to my amazement, I heard the bold theme song to "Back to the Future." I recognized it right away. We owned the video and would pop it in the machine pretty often because it was one of our favorites.

"Bill? We're going in now. I'll talk to you later Honey, and give you a full report. Do you have the tickets, Vito?"

"Got 'em right here."

The son of a bitch! Ever since we got married six years ago Rae and me have talked about going to LA and especially to the Universal Studios Tour to take that ride because we like the movie so much. Now here was some moving man I didn't even know accompanying my wife instead of me.

I was so angry at the thought that for a few seconds I forgot where I was and what had been going on.

"You see Mr. Gallatin, everything is all right. By the time your wife's ride is over, you'll know everything and the two of you will be back home again. But in the meantime she can be having the time of her life. Do something she's always wanted to do. Isn't that super? We try to make everybody happy."

"No it's not super! I was supposed to be there with her! How come Vito gets to go while I'm here with a sore ass talking to you in the dark? Who are you anyway? Can't you turn on some lights?"

"You wouldn't want that. You don't want to see me." He said it quietly and kind of to-himself sad.

"Why's that?"

It was quiet a minute. Then he said something that slammed-shut every door in my head. "Do you ever look in the toilet after you go?"

"What?"

"Sneak a peek at what your body didn't want. Check to see what your stomach set free?"

"For God's sake! That's disgusting."

"Tell the truth now, son."

"You're not my doctor! Why should I tell you that? I've had enough. I want out. How do I open this door?"

"If you open it you'll see me and that will be the end for you." The tone of his voice said this is the truth-- don't doubt it. "I asked about looking in the toilet because in a way that's what I am. I'm everything about yourself you don't like, Mr. Gallatin. I am the shit you look at in the toilet. Once a delicious meal, now just brown stink."

I would have laughed in his face if I could have seen it. But since it was so dark, I barked out a loud phony one to give him the same effect. "You're nuts. And why did you lick me? What was that all about?"

Now he laughed. "That wasn't me—it was your old friend Cyrus. Who's right here next to me. Remember him?"

"No. Who's Cyrus?"

"Why he's your soul, Mr. Gallatin. Don't you recognize it when you are touched by your own soul?"

"My soul's warm and furry and has a tongue like a dog? I don't think so, Mr. Beef-low."

"Beeflow. You disappoint me, sir. Shall I give you a demonstration?"

"You can give me the key out of here."

"All right."

Suddenly the truck door opened—bam and I didn't think twice. I ran for the daylight and jumped off the lip of the back of the truck. Something smart told me don't look back. Was there really a Beeflow or a Cyrus or anything else to further cook my already-barbecued brain? I didn't want to find out. The only thing on my mind at the moment was to get the fuck out of there.

When my feet touched pavement I started running. I was so bent on getting someplace, anyplace away from there that I didn't really look around. Why should I? This was my town. I'd lived here all my life. All I had to do was grab a quick glimpse of what was around me and I'd know exactly where I was. And just when the thought of taking that quick glimpse came to me, I heard something coming up very fast behind me. The sound it made scared me right down to the basement of my blood cells.

And whatever it was got closer while I ran faster, as fast as I could. Just as I cried out 'cause I knew I was caught, doomed, the thing jumped on my back and knocked me flat on my face.

It was heavy. Huge. Whatever hit me had a lot of weight and that fact made it a ton more scary.

So I stayed down, a mouse with a cat on its back, my cheek flat against the hot street asphalt. I could smell it, along with other things. Something in my mouth was bleeding, my nose honked hurt. I tasted blood; pain flew around my face. I smelled the hot street.

"Pose, get down boy. Come back here." The man's voice wasn't familiar but just hearing the thing on my back had a name, a name I understood made me feel sort of better. But "Pose" stayed standing on me and did not move and inch of its heavy self.

"Damn it, dog, what'd I just say to you? Get over here!"

The weight left and I was free again. Looking up a little, I saw four large hairy paws moving away. Slowly I put my palms flat on the ground and pushed myself to my knees. My arms were shaking because I guess I wasn't finished being scared.

"Jeez buddy, I'm terribly sorry about that. Pose gets carried away sometimes when he sees someone running like you were. He wants to get in on the fun. Still pretty much a puppy." The voice tried to be friendly and apologizing at the same time. I was finally going to kick someone's ass: Pose's Daddy. Standing again, I brushed off my hands and looked up real slow, Clint Eastwood- style.

Five feet away a giant Irish wolfhound stood next to a nothing-looking man. Both of them were on fire. I mean, both man and dog were *in big bright flames.* The guy was smiling and came towards me. Before I could do anything he stuck out a burning hand to shake and said, " I'm Mel Shaveetz. Nice to meet you. We just moved in here a couple of days ago. Haven't met many people yet."

Taking one giant step back, I jammed both hands as deep into my pockets as they'd go. Through his flames Mel frowned until it dawned on him. "Oh for God's sake, I'm sorry!" He blew on his index finger. All the flames on him went out like he'd blown out a birthday candle. Like he was blowing himself out.

"I keep forgetting. Sorry about that."

"Who are you?"

Instead of answering, he reached down and squeezed the dog's nose. Its flames went out too. "Mel Shaveetz. And this is Posafega."

"You were on fire!"

"Yeah well, that happens where we come from."

"And where's that?"

"Hell."

"You mean you're dead?"

"Couldn't put on this kind of light show if I was alive. Did you think I was one of those monks who burn themselves alive?"

"You and the dog are dead?"

"No, I am. Pose is just a hound from Hell. He's my roommate."

"A Hell hound!"

"That's right."

"How come I didn't get burned when he was standing on my back?"

"Because you're not dead."

"It just looks like a big wolfhound to me."

Mel shrugged. "Nobody ever said what breed Hellhounds had to be. You want to come in the house and have a beer?"

"Which house do you mean? I know everyone who lives around here."

He pointed to a brown and white saltbox across the street. "You're looking at it—number 88."

"88? I know who lives in 88 and it isn't you. Chris and Terry Rolfe live there."

He looked away and tried to make his eyes busy. "Yeah well, not anymore. They moved."

I remembered what our refrigerator movers had said about seeing piles of people's belongings left out on the street. And I remembered the Brothers saying that was because the dead were being moved back to earth from hell.

"I went to school with Chris Rolfe. He's lived in this town as long as I have. I'd know if he was planning to leave."

"Look, you want that beer or not?"

I wanted to check out the inside of that house. I didn't believe for a minute what he was saying about Rolfe. As far as I knew, that house still belonged to a living guy I saw at least once a week for the past twenty years.

We walked slowly up to the front door, Posafega keeping us company all the way. Not only was that dog big, it was also seriously ugly. Its hair looked like stuffing out of an eighty-year-old mattress. Its face was thin enough to open a letter. The animal was so big that if it stood on its hind legs and had a good hook shot, it could have played pro basketball. So that was a Hellhound. I said the word inside my mouth to myself-- Hellhound.

Just as we were walking in the door, I smelled smoke. Sure enough, Mel was beginning to go up in flames again. "Hey man, you're on fire."

"Yeah well, I'll fix it when we get inside." He kept moving while his flames kept rising. The big dog's too.

Remember I said we love the movie BACK TO THE FUTURE? Well my wife and I are just overall big movie fans so it isn't the only video we own. And that's where my next problem arrived. I wasn't about to pass up the chance to see the inside of a dead man's house and look around for Chris Rolfe. Plus the invitation was offered on a silver platter. But when I think about it now, maybe going in there wasn't the best idea I ever had. Because here's what happened next: Opening the front door, Mel and flame-dog marched in, no big deal. A lot more carefully I followed but got only a few feet into the place before I froze and my jaw dropped below sea level.

I recognized what I saw immediately because I'd seen it so often before and had always wished I could go there. Now I was. The inside of Mel's house, the house that used to belong to Chris Rolfe, was now 'Rick's American Bar' from the movie CASABLANCA.

While my brain tried to swallow that fact, Mel sat down at the white piano and began playing the movie's theme song, "As Time Goes By." He wasn't bad either. Then he began to sing it but I was walking around the room so I didn't pay much attention. The dog plumped down on the floor and went to sleep. I was in such shock that I didn't realize until later that both of them lost their flames as soon as we got into the house. Like once they were home they were normal again. Although my idea of normal that day had taken a vacation to another planet.

As far as I could see every detail in the room was perfect, right down to the ashtrays on the table and full bottles behind the bar. The room was empty except for us, which gave it a whole different feeling from what it was like in the movie. Other than that though, this definitely was Rick's place. If Humphrey Bogart had walked in at that minute I would not have been one bit surprised.

Mel finished playing with a big right hand display—DONG! —and afterwards everything was very quiet in there. Naturally I was tempted to say real coolly "Play it again, Sam" but I didn't.

Instead I asked, "What is all this?"

"It's Rick's. Don't you know CASABLANCA? The movie?"

"Yes I know CASABLANCA! That wasn't my question. How come you live in this house now and it looks like a movie set instead of someone's living room?"

"Before we come back, they ask us what kind of décor we would like where we live. We get to choose."

"Choose what?'"

"The décor! What'd I just tell you?"

"I'm very confused, Mel."

He took a deep breath like I was the stupidest being he'd ever met and my dumbness was using up his air supply. "Before we come back here, to earth, they ask what kind of décor we'd like in the house they assign us. We get to choose. I said Rick's American Bar from the movie because that was the coolest place on earth."

"How long ago did you die?"

"Last Friday."

"How?"

"I drowned in Aqaba, scuba diving. I stepped on a poisonous sea urchin and had an allergic reaction. Pretty pathetic way to go."

"And you went to Hell?"

"Straight to. Do not pass go, do not collect two hundred dollars."

"But you're back here a week later?"

"Not by choice, pal. Not by choice." The doorbell rang. Mel held up one finger for quiet. "Let me just get that. What kind of beer do you want? I've got everything here. There's even a good Polish one. Zee-veetch or some name like that."

He left the room and the animal followed. I wondered if it was some kind of satanic chaperone. What kind of visitors did the dead have? That thought grew so fast and so horror movie-ugly in my head that in the minute or so it took Mel to return, I was almost hyperventilating. What kind of visitors DID the dead have? Good God, what if they were—

"It's for you."

I opened my mouth, closed it, opened again. "Me? No one knows I'm here."

"Yeah well, obviously they do. They say they want to talk to you. Two goofy looking guys with shaggy haircuts."

"Brooks and Zin Zan!"

"Whatever." Mel shrugged.

I started out but stopped short when I thought of something. "Were…were you on fire when they saw you?"

"Sure. Any time I step out of this house I start to burn. One of the many drawbacks of being back on earth again." He sounded angry about it, put out.

"Did you like it in Hell?"

"I can't say much about it because that's against the rules; You being alive and all." He looked left and right, as if some enemy might be listening. "But I will tell you this—ever think maybe that Hell stuff you've always heard is a bunch of crap? Maybe it's given all that bad press because they want to keep people OUT of there? That if people really knew what it was like, an awful lot of them might kill themselves to get there sooner?"

The dog started growling. It was not a sound you ever want to hear. Worse, it was staring at Mel while it snarled. That monster's lip was curled up and twitching like it was going to attack any second.

"Shut up, Pose. How about that cat you told the other day? Don't you think I was listening?"

"Whoa! You and the dog understand each other?"

"Different rules apply when you're dead. Yes we understand each other. He's pissed off at me for telling you about Hell. It doesn't matter. You'd better go see your friends. I'll get the beers." He went to the bar and I left the room.

Sure enough, Brooks and Zin Zan were standing just the other side of the open doorway. They lit up when they saw me. I gotta admit I was happy to see them too, considering everything that had been happening.

"Hi guys, what are you doing here?"

Both opened their mouths and started talking but I didn't hear a thing. Their faces and hand movements were busy too but came with no soundtrack. After a while I pointed to my ears and made a face that said nothing's coming through. They seemed to understand and gestured for me to step outside.

Just as I was about to do exactly that, Mel Shaveetz's voice said from about five inches behind my ear, "I wouldn't go out there if I were you."

Still looking at the Brothers, I asked why not? I don't like being told what to do; especially not by dead people who live on movie sets with burning dogs.

"Because once you do, you can't come back in here again."

"Why would I want to?"

"Because the answers you need are in here, not out there with them." Mel's voice was snotty and know-it-all, all "You dumbbell--I'm smarter than you are" tone. Which I hate. Without even bothering to look back at the asshole, I stepped towards the Brothers. I heard a terrible savage growl from back in the house. The hairy Devil dog was coming for me again.

Adding to that, the Brothers' eyeballs widened till they almost popped out of their heads at whatever it was they saw coming up behind me. Then those holy cowards turned on their four heels and ran. Me too. Not that I expected to get very far. I knew how that giant could run. I'd felt its weight pressing down on my back. Now I knew any second it'd be on me again doing a lot worse than before.

I'm running and know I'll be caught but I'll fight back. What else could I do? For the first sprint I ran looking at the ground. That's how I always ran fastest as a kid. No distractions, just watch the ground straight in front of you and move like lightning in front of thunder.

But eventually I realized even through all the fear that nothing had caught or eaten me yet. So I looked up, wondering why not? The Brothers were a hundred feet ahead, standing still now and facing me.

Why had they stopped when a moment ago they were so scared? And where was that Posafega?

I looked over my shoulder cringing because it might just be waiting to give me a nasty shock. But the only surprise was that that dog wasn't there. "What is going on?"

"We were afraid we wouldn't be able to get you out of there, sir. That would have been big trouble for all concerned. But here you are—you made it!" Zin Zan looked like he was about to kiss me, he was so happy.

Instead of answering, I looked at Rolfe's house again to make sure we were talking about the same thing. Only when I was bringing my eyes back around to the Brothers did I see a street sign: Pilot Hill. That's where we'd been planning to go in the first place before all this other shit started happening.

"Is this what you wanted to show me? Rolfe's house? Is that what this is all about?"

"No sir, actually it was someone else's house we wanted to show you up here. But I don't think you need to see it now to believe what we were saying before."

"True. So who else lost their house on this street?"

They looked at each other to see which of them was going to drop the next bad news bomb. Zin Zan said, "Everyone."

"What?"

"That's right." Brooks moved his arm in a way that took in the whole area. "Every house on Pilot Hill has been taken over."

"I don't believe it." I looked around again to make sure that dog wasn't sneaking up on me from some secret angle.

"It's true, Mr. Gallatin. If you'd like, go look in anyone's window here and you'll see."

"I will do exactly that." I crossed the street to my friend Carl Hull's house and looked in his window because I knew exactly what it looked like inside. What I noticed first was everything was black and white in there. Or I should say in black and white. I knew Carl's house and this wasn't it. I stepped back and looked at the façade. This was Hull's house, all right. So I looked in the window again. Carl's wife Naomi loves yellow things—furniture, pillows, rugs. But there wasn't an inch of yellow anything in there. No couch, curtains, nothing-- only black and white.

The living room was full of old fat furniture; most of it covered in some thick material like velvet. Like your Grandma's house. Pure old people's furniture. The Hull house I knew had a few pieces of cheap yellow furniture, a round "Garfield" rug in front of a TV set as big as you could get. That machine was Carl's pride and you had to give the man credit—he didn't scrimp when it came to home entertainment. But where was that big Sony screen today?

"Sherlock Holmes."

I jumped. "Don't do that, Brooks! Don't sneak up on me. My eggs have been scrambled enough for one day. Besides, what are you talking about?"

"This house--The woman who moved in here chose the decor of the first Sherlock Holmes film. Starring Clive Brook, Ernest Torrence-"

"Where's Carl and Naomi?"

"At Lake of the Ozarks on vacation. They'll be coming back soon to this ugly surprise."

"Where's their stuff? Their belongings?"

"The new tenant had it hauled away this morning."

"Why is everything in black and white in there?"

Brooks seemed surprised at my question. "Because that film was in black and white. The new occupant wanted things to look exactly like the film."

"Well, CASABLANCA was black and white too. But Mel's house was in color. You saw it."

Brooks nodded. "He chose the colorized version. He's not a purist. I hope you don't mind me saying this, Mr. Gallatin, but it would be very good if we got a move on."

"Where to now?"

"Back to your house."

"What's at my house that wasn't there an hour ago?"

"A moving van."

Three sets of eyes bounced back and forth, back and forth like "Flubber" for a while before any of the mouths connected to them had more to say.

"They're taking over my house now?"

"Yes sir. That's why we came to warn you this morning."

"You knew about this? You knew it would happen?" We started walking—fast.

"We always know it'll happen-- Just not when. We didn't think it would be so soon and in such large numbers. That's why we go door to door. The problem is no one ever believes what we say until it's too late. So Beeflow decided to change the way we do things because the situation is now getting critical."

"Was that really Beeflow who talked to me back in the truck?"

"Yes sir. Was Cyrus there too?"

"How do you know about that? I thought it was my soul!"

"It is. Did it lick your hand in the dark?" He smiled and shook his head like he'd just found a fond memory in his pocket. "That's its way of greeting you, telling you it's there. It happens that way to us all. But 'Cyrus' is only Beeflow's nickname for it. The real name of the human soul is Kopum, pronounced Coe-poom. You'll learn all about that later."

"Then why does he call it Cyrus?"

"It's easier to accept in the beginning. The name sounds a lot less strange than Kopum. People like feeling safe, especially when it comes to their souls."

We hurried back and only when we were halfway home did I think about what I was doing or the fact I had accepted everything they'd told me as cold hard fact. The name of my soul was Cyrus, but not really because it's actually Kopum. Okay. Dead people were moving into my house? If you say so. The craziness of it all made me slow some but not stop. I'd seen and heard enough in the last hour to know parts of my world had suddenly gone seriously damned wobbly, but this? Could it really be true?

"Look at that."

I was so deep into thinking about all of this that my brain didn't click until my eyes saw the scene in front of us. And then the first thing I did was burst out laughing. There's this guy I know and work with named Eric Dickey. Just saying that name makes my lips squinch up like I ate something bad. I hate that son of a bitch. You don’t want to get me started on him because I’ve got a whole alphabet of reasons why I do not wish him well-- in this life or any other. It’s enough to say that we started disliking each other in ninth grade and only got better at it as the years passed.

Anyway, Eric Dickey and his stumpy wife Sue live in a nice house a few blocks from ours. And I’ve got to admit it is a handsome place. Eric is a foreman at my company who knows how to kiss ass well enough to get promotions while the rest of us are worrying half the time about what will happen if there are layoffs. But the fact of the matter is the Dickeys do have a really nice house and at work Eric is always bragging about the new this or new that they bought for their place. They don't have any kids so they go all- out buying top of the line air conditioners, lawnmowers, gas grills… the kind of expensive things that can be seen from the street and coveted by the rest of us slobs. A real asshole.

So anyway I'm laughing now because what do you know-- old Dickey's stuff is piled on the street in front of his beautiful house. This time seeing a pile like that doesn't surprise me so much as make my heart throw a fist in the air and yell ALL RIGHT! Maybe this Hell business isn't so bad after all. But that feeling was short- lived because just as I was relishing seeing kiss-ass Dickey's stuff dumped out on the street, who should walk around from the back of his house but a cave-man!

So help me God. That sounds totally nuts but it is the truth. And you've seen him before in every caveman movie you ever watched. The fucker is hunched over in a sort of monkey scrunch and has got so much hair growing on his body that you can't really make out where the head ends and the rest begins. I mean this fellow is ALL hair and even when he looks at you, his face is hard to make out because everything is so completely covered in fur.

Now if that wasn't enough, this whatever it is, this creature looks at us and growls like a monster. No, he more like roars like a lion and it's one loud ugly sound. Then he threw up two furry arms that looked like a couple of tree trunks with brown moss growing off them. I was sure he was going to come charging at us because he thought we were going to steal his place from him. But as far as I was concerned, he was the best neighbor in town if he had evicted Eric Dickey on his bragging ass.

When I thought for sure Mr. Caveman was coming for us, I put up my hand-- palm out. I was even about to say "How!" like cowboys do to Indians when they meet up on the prairie. Where that idea came from in my brain I do not know, except maybe I thought you greeted dinosaur eaters the same way you did Commanches. Even though the two groups were only about a few million years apart on the time line.

When he roared again I thought it was time to get out of there so I started off.

"Wait, don't run. He can't bother you." Zin Zan called out.

I stopped but my feet weren't convinced. They kept going up and down, sort of running in place just in case he was wrong. "How do you know that?"

"Because we're with you. We know how to keep him away. You're protected so long as you don't go into his house. That's why it was so dangerous when you went into that other man's place."

"But where's Dickey and his wife?"

"Hiding in their basement."

"No shit?" Ear to ear I was grinning. Ear to ear.

"You're going to have to stop using that kind of language, Mr. Gallatin. It just won't do."

I wanted to say fuck you, but the picture of Eric hiding in his basement from a furry caveman, while all his high-priced possessions sat in a heap on the curb… that was happiness enough for the moment to keep my dirty words in my mouth. "So dead people from all the different ages are being sent back here? Not just recent ones like Mel?"

Brooks shook his head and frowned. "That is correct. It's totally chaotic but only part of the problem we face. Look! That is exactly what I'm talking about!" From behind the house smoke and flame started coming around the corner. And not just "too many burgers on the barbecue" stuff—these were big impressive clouds of brown smoke and some yellow flame coming fast and scary towards us.

"What's happening?"

Zin Zan pointed at the caveman. "He probably started a fire back there. He can't help it—guys like him don't know any better."

"Should we do something about it?"

From the distance came faint siren sounds.

"No, someone's obviously called it in already. We've got to get to your house now."

"Yeah, but what's going to happen when the firetrucks get here and have to deal with Mr. One Million B.C.?" I pointed at you-know-who.

"That's their problem, not ours. Right now we've got to get you back home."

We started walking again but I kept turning around to look at that hairy guy standing in front of Eric's house. He didn't move. Smoke was coming thick and fast behind him but he didn't move. The sirens got louder, nearer. Were those voices coming from inside the house? Was someone shouting in there?

"Come on, Mr. Gallatin. There's no time."

I looked at the Brothers. I looked at the caveman. I looked at the house, the smoke behind him. I knew I was about to do something really stupid and probably unnecessary.

"We can't just go."

Both Brothers turned towards the siren sounds and gestured toward them. "They're coming now. They'll be here any minute."

"But what happens in the meantime? Maybe they'll die down there of smoke inhalation or whatever. Don't you watch those emergency rescue shows on TV? Every minute counts."

"Every minute counts for you too. You have to save your home! Do you understand that? *They are taking your house!*"

I lowered my head and started walking in the wrong direction. One of them touched my arm. I shook him off. Eric Dickey was a turd but I wasn't going to let him die. Maybe I was being stupid because he probably would have been saved just fine without my help. But I don't want ugly things on my conscience. I don't want to live the rest of my life with a picture pinned to the inside of my brain of a man and his weasel eyed wife lying face down forever in a smoky basement because I needed to get home.

"We won't be able to help if you go in there. We can't go with you!"

"Then just wait out here. I'll be right back." I kept walking. The caveman saw me but seemed to have his mind on other things. He lifted his head and sniffed the air like an animal—nose up high, making these little up and down jerks every now and again. Sniff—jerk-sniff-jerk. Then he turned and ran around the house to the back.

Which was just fine with me because it gave me free access to the front door. The moment B.C. disappeared from sight, I ran for it. Behind me the Brothers were hollering now "Don't!" and "Please come back!" But I was already there. The bad news was that door was locked. The good news? An aluminum baseball bat was leaning against the house. Without a second's hesitation I picked it up. Not a second too soon because I heard a rough animal grunt behind me. Not too close but close enough to have me bringing that bat up to 'play ball!' height by the time I'd swiveled around to face that grunt. In shock I almost dropped the damned thing seeing what I did.

The caveman was about ten feet away. In his hands was the charred body of what could only have been a dog. In fact it was definitely a dog because the head wasn't as grilled as the rest of the black still-smoking body. I could make out that it was once upon a time a beagle or some such. That's what the fire behind the house probably started off being: He was cooking some poor sucker's Lassie or

Snoopy. Rest in Peace, Snoop. Bet you never thought you'd end up lunch.

I didn't have any time to think about it because B.C. dropped his Happy Meal and came at me. I swung the bat at his head. Lucky for him, he was able to turn a bit at the last second so instead of hitting a homerun I only knocked him flat.

The clang of metal-on-head sounded like a cooking pot dropped on concrete. I knew I hadn't killed him because he was already dead, but also because he was twitching and frothing up ugly stuff out at the mouth. I stood over him a few seconds to see if he'd get up again. But most of him was on vacation and what wasn't, was busy jerking around.

So I swung that fine silver bat again, this time through one of the large windows into what I assumed was the Dickey living room. After the first crash of glass, I knocked out some slivers still stuck in the window frame and after a last glance at him just to be sure, I climbed in.

I've never been to a jungle. I've never been most places but that's okay because I don't speak other languages and the idea of a passport makes me nervous. But as soon as I put both feet down inside the Dickey's house I was hit by a wet tropical heat the likes of which I'd never experienced. Everything around me was like this 3-D green. A green so strong it almost hurt my eyes. When I took a step forward, I was hit in the face by some kind of nasty thick vine that was a whole new scare in itself. When I managed to push that out of the way I tried to get my bearings looking left and right but all I saw was green eve-rything and sounds that screamed and screeched and cawed and pretty much made me deaf. I was in a jungle somehow and as that sunk into my brain I somehow remembered a line from school that just popped up out of nowhere but said it all—the forest primeval.

Mel Shaveetz had said they got to choose a décor when they came back to earth. So of course a caveman would want one exactly like where he had been living. In the forest primeval. The earth a million years ago or fifty thousand or whenever.

Instead of Eric Dickey's living room, I was back on earth a zillion years ago, standing like a rabbit frozen in its headlights. And there were no walls in this "décor"; it wasn't limited to a few closed-in rooms like Rick's Bar. Everywhere I looked was jungle that went out in every direction with no end in sight. This wasn't a room—this was forever. Right about then the next words came to my mind.

"Jurassic Park." I said out loud but couldn't hear very well for all the screeching going on around me.

"Dinosaurs!" Monsters with teeth as big as the baseball bat I still held. Walking houses with serious appetites for anything fleshy. I had to get out of here. In a panic I turned around, planning to go right back through the window into my world. But there was no window. Only trees and vines and green and noise.

Eventually my brain stopped its own screeching in fear. And although I was scared shitless of what might come stomping out of the trees at any minute, I was losing control so fast that there was only one thing left to do—close my eyes. A trick that almost always worked for me when things got so bad I could feel life unraveling. Close my eyes and say, "I am driving my life. I am steering this car. I CONTROL THINGS."

I started the "I am-" but it was drowned out by the terrible new sound of something very big-- and near-- coming my way through the jungle. THUMP THUMP THUMP. It was running! As huge as it sounded in the not so far distance, the speed of its footsteps said it was running at me. It was my turn to be lunch.

"What are the six questions?"

How did I hear that? The voice had spoken calmly and in no hurry. But I heard it clearly above everything else. What six questions? Who was this? Were they the last words I'd ever hear? WAS IT GOD?

"No, Mr. Gallatin, it's Beeflow. What are the six questions?"

Thump Thump Thump. I heard bushes crashing, birds crying out like they do when they're disturbed or attacked. This monster was closer, it was almost here.

'WHAT ARE THE SIX QUESTIONS?"

"I don't know what the fuck you're talking about! Get me out of here!"

And then the biggest shock of all—I heard him sigh! A disappointed sigh. The sigh of a teacher when you've answered a question wrong in class.

"All right, I'll help you this one time but not again. Name one experience from your past you wish you could repeat. That is the third question."

"Are you nuts? Now? The thing's coming! Get me out of here."

"Then answer the question, and quickly."

"An experience I want to repeat? I don't know. Jeez, I don't know. Help me, willya?" My voice sounded like one of the scared birds up in the trees.

"No, help yourself—answer that question."

And when he said that, an answer came so clear and calm to my mind that I was surprised I hadn't known it immediately. "I wish I could have sex again for the first time with Rae. That was the best night of my life."

"Very very good. Now look in your hand."

I looked, even though the bushes nearby rustled hard which meant whatever monster was coming had arrived. Instead of the silver baseball bat, I held a black metal cylinder about two feet long. The dinosaur burst out at me like a rocket with legs. Its teeth were even bigger than I had thought they'd be. Its open mouth looked ten feet wide. I didn't even have a chance to raise the cylinder up to do whatever it might do to fight off the thing. Because it was there.

And then gone.

That's right--it whizzed right by me. Whatever kind of prehistoric piece of shit it was, the creature ran by and went crashing on into the jungle behind me. It didn't even stop to have a look or say hello. Not that I was disappointed. I stood there looking after it and then I looked at the black cylinder in my hand, trying to figure out how it played into all of this. No answer came. It was just this metal thing that a while before had been a baseball bat.

I stood there listening while Tyrannosaurus-whatever galloped farther away into the jungle. And then it became quiet around me, or as quiet as a place like that is ever going to be. It took me some more time to de-tox from the scare that was still sending fireballs of adrenaline to all corners of my body. I stood a while longer and then sort of collapsed on the ground in a heap, dropping the cylinder as I did.

I looked at it and wondered what kind of magic had changed it from a baseball bat into this without my ever having felt it. I wondered if it had somehow saved me from being eaten. Or had answering Bee-flow's question been the reason? What were these six questions he was talking about? What was this cylinder lying on the ground a foot away? How was I going to get out of the forest primeval and back to my world?

"Don't turn around."

I didn't but sure was tempted. It was Beeflow again. "Why can't I look at you?"

"Because I told you before, Mr. Gallatin, I am everything ugly about you. I'm your shit in the toilet, the dark side of your moon, the worst lies you've told, the hurt you dropped on others. I am everything bad about you and if you want to look that square in the face then go ahead. But I warn you, looking your own evil in the eye is as bad as looking at Medusa. It will wreck you, turn part of you into stone."

"And you say you're me?"

"Only in part. I've chosen to take on all that's bad in you for the time being so that you can face challenges other than your own."

"Are you, uh, human?"

"I was once, but am no longer. Years ago I had a vision and it changed me forever."

"What kind of vision?"

"You're looking at it now."

I happened to be looking at the cylinder next to me. "That thing? The baseball bat?"

"Yes. I was in a flea market in London and on a table amongst other junk was a brass object. I worked as a travel agent but my great hobbies were inventing and the history of tools. So I was well versed in the function of all sorts of machinery, archaic tools, and the like. I was no newcomer to obscure gadgets. But for the life of me I could not understand what purpose this gizmo served. Written on the side of it in thick letters were the words 'Heidelberg Cylinder.' I picked it up and turned it over and over in my hands but its purpose still baffled me. I was perplexed and fascinated, so I paid three pounds and put it in my pocket.

"When I returned home to America and was able to look through the reference books in my library, I discovered something staggering: The Heidelberg Cylinder had been used in every great modern invention. The cotton gin, the first steam engine, the telephone, internal combustion engine… You name it and a version of the cylinder was one of the components. It was the essential piece in every one of those innovations. It was the thing that made them all work. I was astonished and then utterly skeptical so I researched further. Different versions of the cylinder were used in the first telegraph, the television, computers. Sometimes it was made of a different metal, or Bakelite, then plastic, carbon… you get the point. It was the part that made these earth-shaking inventions work Mr. Gallatin, but no one had ever noted the connection. One man made object made all of these things possible.

"I couldn't believe that no one had ever made the discovery. And then it hit me—no one was <u>supposed</u> to make the discovery! The

Heidelberg Cylinder is meant to be invented again and again in its different guises and then put into the workings of whatever new different machines we dream up in the future.

"Because do you know what the cylinder really is? The concrete proof of our immortality. The result of the human mind and spirit working as one to solve problems and overcome them. Any problems. Physical proof of the fact we can do anything we want, even live forever if we choose, if we set our minds to it."

I looked at it and rubbed my mouth. "That thing?"

"Yes, that thing."

I picked it up, turned it over. It was black and there was nothing written on it. Definitely not any "Heidelberg Cylinder."

"How come it's black then and there's no writing on it?"

"Because once you realize what it is, it changes into something else. Something someone else will need to discover its importance. For me it was the brass object I described. For the person who had it before you it turned into a 16th century Persian lock. For you it became a baseball bat."

"Then what is it now?"

"I don't know. Probably something from the future."

Reaching out to pick it up, I stopped when he said that. "But I didn't discover anything with the baseball bat. Definitely not any of that stuff you were saying about man's immortality: I just brained the caveman with it."

"Yes but that's because I've chosen to intervene. There simply isn't enough time for it to happen in the slow and proper way it should. Mankind is in jeopardy and we must work quickly to avoid a catastrophe. I'll tell you the end of my story briefly and then you will understand.

"When I grasped the extraordinary importance of the Heidelberg Cylinder, I became obsessed with my search and found it again and again the further I looked. But what was I to do with my discovery? Who should I tell and in what context?"

I had to interrupt. "When did you turn into, uh, what you are?"

"Once we've learned about the Cylinder, all of us change eventually."

That made me stand up. "What do you mean? Change how?"

"It varies from person to person. I can't say how it will affect you."

I was getting nervous again. "But what about Brooks and Zin Zan? They're both normal. They're weird but they're normal."

"For now because both of them are new to the group. But sooner or later they will change and take on new forms. We call it 'hatching.' As I said, I can't tell you what forms either of them will take, but they will definitely metamorphose into something entirely different."

"Do they know that? Do they know they're going to change?"

"Of course Mr. Gallatin, and they welcome it."

"So that means now that I know, I'm going to change too?"

"Yes."

"But I don't want to change! I like my life."

"I'm afraid we need you more than you need your life. I want to show you something."

Before I had a chance to protest, everything changed. In an instant, a blink, half a breath, we went from jungle to paradise.

I'd heard it before but now I know it's true: paradise is what you want it to be. If you imagine angels with wings and harps sitting on gold clouds, that's what you'll see. Perfect gardens where lions dance the cha-cha while beautiful women serve you ice cold rum? Then that's what it will be. I didn't know my paradise until I saw it. The moment I did, I knew this was it-- Nothing could be better.

An outdoor restaurant in the middle of the countryside somewhere. A few metal tables were set up under four big chestnut trees. The wind was blowing, tossing up the corners of the white tablecloths. The sun shone down through the leaves, flickering beautiful yellow, green and white light across everything.

A bunch of people were sitting at one of the tables having the best time laughing, eating and talking. A black guy was sitting at one end of the table playing a Gibson "Hummingbird" guitar softly but really well. A woman nearby kept jumping up from her place, hugging him and then sitting back down again.

The different colors and variety of food spread out for them across the table was amazing. All kinds of meats and salads, vegetables piled high, soups, cakes and pies. The breads alone would have kept you busy for days making sandwiches. Once you saw it you couldn't take your eyes off this…plenty. My mouth started watering. I knew it had to be the greatest food that ever was and to taste any bit of it would bring you to tears.

"Hey Bill, why're you standing over there like you're hypnotized? Get your ass over here and say hello." The man who spoke didn't just look my father, it was him. He'd been dead eleven years.

I didn't move but just assumed Beeflow was nearby so I asked out loud, "Is it real? Is that really my Dad?"

"Yes. Look around the table. You know everyone there."

It was true. A girl I'd known and liked who'd died in a water skiing accident, my Uncle Birmy next to my father, others. I did know everyone at that table. Some better than others but I had known them all-- when they were alive. When my father called out my name they looked over and smiled like seeing me was the best thing that had happened to them all day. It made me feel good and gave me the damned creeps at the same time.

"Welcome to Hell, Mr. Gallatin," Beeflow said.

Why did I already know that? How did I know that's what he was going to say and it wouldn't surprise me?

"It's the most wonderful place in the world because it's your most wonderful place. Everything is familiar here, you know everyone, the food is gorgeous-"

He was interrupted by the sound of the drowned girl laughing. It was the most beautiful, innocent, sexy laugh I'd ever heard. Her head was thrown back and she was laughing and all I could focus on was her long slim neck. Like everything else there, it was almost too much to take. Since when could the sight of a woman's bare neck send me over the moon?

"You see, it's already beginning to affect you. That's what's so splendid about it. Because everything here is yours, it would be so easy to slide right into this world and never want to go home."

"It really is Hell? This is where you go when you've been bad?"

"Yes. That's what Mel Shaveetz was saying to you and why the dog started growling at him. If people knew how marvelous this is, do you think they'd work hard at living? Or at being good, achieving something, working for one another? Too many of them would throw up their hands and just wait to die. Or they would kill themselves for the stupidest reasons just so they could come here earlier than planned."

"Everyone's Hell is this good?"

"Yes it is."

"Then what's Heaven like?"

"Infinitely better. But it is extremely hard to get into Heaven, Mr. Gallatin. It is almost impossible."

"But a person wins either way: Hell is great and Heaven is better."

"That should make no difference to you when you're alive. There is a purpose to living that is far more important than ending up comfortably dead."

"So what is the purpose of living?"

The people at the table seemed to have forgotten I was standing there and had gone back to enjoying their party. Some of them were singing now. The black guy was playing The Lovin' Spoonful song 'Coconut Grove.' Others were eating big fat chicken legs or steaks;

slices of pie a la mode. More than anything I wanted to go over and join them. Like a hungry kid, I was itching to be at that table.

"Pay attention Gallatin! Stop drooling over hamburgers. What I'm telling you is vitally important. People are alive because they have jobs to do. They are meant to improve and broaden the human experience as best they can. The Cylinder is concrete proof of that. After death, mankind comes here if they've failed, or to Heaven if they succeeded. But if they knew about this, it would change everything. Dangerously few people would work hard, or dream, or love well and with all their hearts. Because no matter how they lived, they get this in the end.

"Mankind's progress has been slow but steady. But now Satan is attempting to change that. He says there is no more room in Hell and has begun moving the dead back to earth in greater and greater numbers. Those who have already been sent were told the move wouldn't be permanent. Life on earth is made as pleasant as possible for them by allowing them to create their environment.

"God cannot reason with Satan about this, but we know that is nothing new. This forced relocation has been going on for centuries, but until now God overlooked it because the few that were sent back to earth were regarded by the living as lunatics and ignored. Not anymore."

"Why? Why is it happening?"

"Because Mankind no longer accepts the idea of Damnation. He no longer feels he deserves eternal suffering for what he did or did not do on earth. Guilt has grown obsolete. In the past, people were so afraid of what would happen to them in the afterlife that they created the most frightening scenarios possible. So when they did die, naturally those things happened to them. They brought their worst nightmares along and they came true.

“No longer. For the common man today, a fire and brimstone Hell has become an old-fashioned idea, and Heaven is a child's dream."

"Because we live happier lives, we get to be happier dead?"

"Exactly, and Satan absolutely hates that. When suffering prevailed in Hell, he was satisfied. But since people create their own Hell from what they knew in life, in recent decades it has generally become a rather nice place. He cannot abide that. So he has changed the rules. He is sending the dead back to earth en masse. And it is clear what affect that will have on things there.”

“Why doesn’t God stop him?”

“Because God wants us to stop him. It is part of our ongoing task.”

“How? How are we supposed to stop the Devil?”

“We must come up with a plan. Perhaps many plans before one works effectively. Obviously some of them will work, others won’t.”

“Jeez Bill, are we going to have to drag you over to the table with a rope? We even got your favorite over there—potato salad with extra horseradish in the sauce.” My father was suddenly standing in front of me smiling that great old smile that had always made me want to climb in his lap and stay there forever.

“Dad, where’s Mom? Is she here?”

He smiled and threw a thumb over his shoulder for me to look there. Coming out of the restaurant was my mother. A cry rose up in my throat that I was just barely able to hold onto before it spilled out. There she was, looking like she did before the cancer ate her body. There she was in that red and white striped dress, all her black hair long and curly again. Best of all she was chubby like before-- "Pleasantly plump" as she called herself. Not the hairless stick-thin woman who turned to the wall one day while lying in her bed and never really turned back, choosing instead to disappear into her sickness and never come out again.

In her hands she held a whipped cream cake. Sort of pale pink on the sides, black bittersweet chocolate on the top. It was my favorite. She had always made it on special occasions. The last time I ever had it was on our wedding day. Rae got the recipe from her but was never able to make it right. All Moms have one secret recipe that can't be copied and this was hers. A whipped cream cake.

She went to the table and put it down in front of an empty seat. Reaching over, she arranged the silverware there. I knew she was setting it up for me. Come over and cut your cake she was saying. Sit with your father and me and tell us what your life has been since we left. Tell us about Rae who we always liked and your job and how you've filled your days. Because we love you and want to hear everything. How many people on this earth want to hear everything about you? How many people-

"They're dead. Mr. Gallatin."

I blinked, looking from my mother to my father. I was in a trance. My mother, my father, her cake, this place-

"They're dead and you have things to do."

Beeflow's words struck my head like a hammer. They hurt that much. I didn't want to hear them; I didn't want this picture of my good parents to go away just because they were dead.

"What do you want from me? It's my parents! I haven't seen them-- Can't I have five minutes together with my parents?"

"You're finding reasons to stay here. And the longer you stay, the more reasons you'll find. It's very tricky that way. Very seductive. But everything here is from your life, Gallatin, it is from life, do you understand? How lucky you've been to amass all these fine memories. How good life has been to you. It's been a good friend. Don't you owe it something?"

Furious, I turned towards his voice without thinking. And when I saw him, when I saw what he was I began to cry. Because he'd told the truth—he was everything I didn't want to know about myself. He had no special shape or size. You couldn't say it's a man or a monster or a Devil or whatever. He was just it, them, all those things you try to ignore or cover up or argue against or justify or put up a million defenses against just to keep from saying there I am, that is part of me.

But then something amazing happened and I don't even know if I can take credit for it. I turned away. I turned away from Mr. Beeflow and looked back at that table, my parents, and the things that made my life big rather than small and shitty. I saw the good people, the good stuff on the table, the trees blowing in the wind and the smell of spring and food and life… Despite having "seen" Beeflow, I still had managed to survive and bring all of these beautiful things along to the death that would some day be mine. I was grateful. And I knew he was right—painful as it was, I had to give all this up for now and go back to do what I could to try and keep life as it had always been for everybody.

"Son?" Dad's voice.

I closed my eyes. "All right, Mr. Beeflow, I understand. Take me back."

Immediately something warm and familiar licked my hand. This time I didn't open my eyes. Whatever it was took the hand and pulled it gently to the left. Blind, I walked a few steps, trusting it, knowing that it was Cyrus. It made so much sense—once you made your mind up to go, only your own soul could lead you back to where you began.

"Not so fast, Monsieur. Who's going to pay for this meal, Bill? The bill, Bill. When you eat at my table, you pay for my cooking."

The Devil wore a chef's cap. One of those stupid high white ones that look like something put on the end of a lamb chop at a ritzy restaurant. He wore that white hat and all the rest of his clothes were white too. His face was nothing special—just a face surrounded by lots of white. No, that's not true—there was one strange- looking thing about him—he had two moustaches. Slim little things, they sat one right under the other like lines on a paper.

"I see by your admiring eye that you're looking at my moustaches. Is this going to be the new trend or what?"

"It looks stupid if you ask me. Plus people can't grow two moustaches."

He shrugged and played with both of them. Top one, then the bottom. "But they can grow one really thick one and cut a space in the middle, making levels."

"It's still stupid."

"Every fool's entitled to his opinion. But let's get back to the facts—how do you plan on paying for this meal? PS I don't take VISA or Mastercard." He laughed and it sounded like someone unscrewing a tight plastic-on-plastic cap. I squinted at the sound but didn't look away. I guess my face said I was confused, so he took my arm. I tried to pull away but he wouldn't let me.

"You chose to come here, Bill boy, and now you want to leave which however is a human no-no. Any person who sees this and wants to go back has to pay."

"Pay with what?"

"Something you love. I'll let you go back but the price for this meal, this little view you just had, is something you love in life. If you stay here you get to keep all this. But if you go back you've got to give me something from you life you never thought you could live without."

"Mr. Beeflow, are you there? Is this true?"

"Forget it, he can't help you. Anyway you saw what he looked like."

"You made Beeflow do this too?"

"Yup. He gave up his body. He was a handsome man. A very vain one too. Nothing he liked more than looking at himself in a mirror and admiring the view. I never thought he would do it but sometimes people surprise me."

Suddenly I remembered Cyrus and looked down at the hand he had been holding. No Cyrus--nothing was there. Only the ground. The ground in this beautiful Hell. Gathering myself together, gathering words in my mouth to make a sentence I never thought I would say in a million years, I took a deep breath and said, "Rae, take my love for Rae."

He didn't react immediately. He looked at me hard, like I was trying to trick him. But we both knew there was no way I could trick him.

"I thought you'd say something like that but it's not enough, Bill. Try again."

"I don't know anything else. That's about as bad as I can imagine. Not loving my wife anymore? What could be worse than not loving Rae?"

I climbed through the window of Eric Dickey's house back out into my world and my life. The first thing I smelled there was big thick smoke. It took only a second to remember I'd gone in there in the first place to save Eric and his wife from burning up in the caveman's fire. Jumping off the porch, I ran around to the back of the house. There was a high pile of wood and other things burning in the middle of their yard. Firemen had a hose turned on it, trying to get it under control. Both of the Dickeys were off to one side on their knees, taking oxygen. There was so much tussle and turmoil out there—people running around, fire being fought, police, firemen and the like. No one noticed me standing there. I couldn't help thinking that there had been absolutely no reason for me to go into that house because the fire had all been out here. But then if I hadn't gone in…

"Brother Bill?"

Brooks came up on one side of me, Zin Zan the other. Neither of them was smiling and neither was I.

"Are you all right?"

A fireman rushed by us and knocked into me hard as he passed but I didn't react.

"Now I'm your Brother? Is that what you call me from now on? Brother Bill?"

"We don't have to call you anything if that's what you'd prefer. Are you all right?"

"You know where I just was, don't you?"

They both nodded.

"And you both were there once and saw the Devil?"

Again, slow nods.

In the smoke and the fire and the confusion and the running around and the noise that was a hundred kinds of noise, I saw something I hadn't seen all afternoon although it had been right in front of me the whole time.

"My God, you're Brooks Collins!"

Half a smile crossed Brother Brooks's face and then died. He nodded again.

"I have all your albums."

"Better take care of them—there won't be any more."

"You gave <u>that</u> up?" A few beats passed until I understood. "That's what you gave the Devil? Your talent?"

"And the fame. He wasn't going to let me go just giving up the one. The world today is full of people who have no talent but are famous. No one recognizes me anymore. Only you, but that's because you've been to Hell. You perceive things other people don't."

"I guess we'd better get going."

It was not a far walk to my place but long enough to look around and appreciate things like I never had before. Now and then we'd pass a house and from just a glimpse, we knew if it had been taken over or not. But once I wasn't sure and crept to a window to look. I can't tell you how happy I was to see a normal family inside watching TV and eating popcorn.

"How come Mel Shaveetz and his dog were on fire when they left their house, but the caveman wasn't? All of them were dead."

"Because the Devil keeps changing the rules all the time. That's the reason why so many people are unhappy in life—the rules keep changing. There's really no way of knowing what will happen from one day to the next with this. That's why it's so hard for us to convince people of what's going on. And because it's happening so much faster now, that's why Beeflow has become more directly involved."

"Why doesn't the Devil stop him?"

"Arrogance. He doesn't see Beeflow or us as a threat. There's your house. Do you know what you're gonna do?"

"Stay here. I've got to see something."

They stood by a light pole while I went and opened the front door. Closing it quietly behind me as if someone nearby was sleeping and I didn't want to wake them, I just stood in the hallway a minute, being home, breathing home. My mother used to say after we'd come back from a trip, "At home, even the walls heal you." And that's just how I felt standing there, smelling my life in those near rooms, my eyes running over our possessions and photos on the walls that I knew the whole history of. Lucky me-- all of them showed in different ways what a very good time I'd had right up until that day. Lucky me. But the Brothers had earlier said a moving van had been in front of my house. That's why I'd come back in here-- to see who had taken over our house and how they had changed things. I needed to see what was different so I could prepare my wife and somehow protect her from what was happening. But why then was nothing different in here?

Then I heard it-- the zhunk of furniture being shoved hard across a floor. Someone else was in my house. Someone upstairs from the sound of it. The back of my neck prickled and my eyes opened wide of their own doing. I wore sneakers so I was able to cross the floor and climb the stairs with very little sound. While climbing I heard that same sound a few more times, sometimes louder and longer, sometimes short and sharp. Zhunk-silence-zhuuunk. Like that. I couldn't figure out what it was but it was definitely real and I needed to find out about it.

At the top of the stairs I stood still and waited till the next time it came. It was down the hall in our bedroom. Zhunk. From where I stood I could see that door was open about a third and something white was on the floor just inside the bedroom. I couldn't make out what it was. Tiptoeing down the hall, I kept trying to focus in on what that white thing was. It came to me in stages. A piece of clothing--a shirt-- a white T-shirt. And just when I realized that's what it was, I heard the other sounds. Sex. A woman having sex and liking it a lot.

Rae doesn't like sex. That's been the major problem in our marriage. Once in a while she's sort of in the mood, but it's like when you're sort of in the mood for pizza but can easily do without it if there's none around. I always get the feeling she's doing me a favor when she says yes and I can’t tell you how dry and lonely that makes me feel. She’s a woman I have always wanted to touch but it is more than clear she doesn’t want that.

A T-shirt was on the floor and when I looked I saw writing on it and knew it said ‘Hard Rock Café’. It was my shirt but it was very big and Rae liked that so she often slept in it. Her sounds kept up and they would have made any man hot. I’d known them once but not for a long time. Still, I recognized them instantly. I walked as close to the door as I could and looked in.

My wife was on our bed naked, straddling a guy who’s face I couldn’t see. She was working him so hard that their banging bodies made the bed slide on the floor. Zhunk.

Even when we did have sex, she’d never do it like that with me because she didn’t like me seeing her whole naked. It was always in the dark and she’d wear some kind of clothes—a shirt or sweatshirt so she’d never be completely stripped. As if wearing something meant she was still distant from me and this act even when it was going on.

Did I watch? Yes. Did it make me hot? It sure did. I stood off to a side and watched her do to whoever was beneath her all the things I’d dreamt of her doing with me for as long as I could remember.

What had I given to the Devil to come back here? Rae’s love for me. My love for her wasn’t enough, or so he said. So I said take hers then.

Our relationship wasn't the best. We never had sex anymore, and we seemed to fight more than we should have. Still, I knew she loved me in her scared, mysterious way. I could see it in her eyes when she looked at me sometimes. Plus there were other things she did that overall made up for what was missing. You get along and sometimes you get along so well that you don't think about what you're missing because you just love them there in your life, whatever way they've chosen to be.

As I stood there watching my wife fuck another man, I knew the Devil had changed the rules again: no dead people had moved into my house. No Casablanca backgrounds or jungles were needed here. Everything was the same except for the fact my wife's love for me was dead. What more proof did I need than what was right in front of me?

There was nothing to take. I turned and went back down the hall, down the stairs. I was planning to go right back out of the house but when I touched the front doorknob I stopped. I walked back to the kitchen and without thinking, kissed that new refrigerator. The thing that had started all this in the first place. That was all I wanted to do before leaving but don't ask me why. It just meant something to me and that was reason enough. I kissed our silver refrigerator and it was cool metal on my lips and then it was really time to go.

"Mr. Gallatin?" Beeflow's voice.

I stood and stared at the refrigerator. "What?"

"If it's of any comfort, he didn't make this happen. It's been going on for some time. Upstairs?"

"*I know what you mean.*"

"You were never supposed to know about it. She was always very careful and discreet. But when you offered it to him, when you gave up her love for you-"

"I know what you're saying, Beeflow. I'm not that stupid. He shows me the truth, you show me the truth... Both of you are killing me with all this truth about my life. Was that the plan? Because what good does it do? Seeing the truth just shows you how wrong you were about things and how ugly they really are."

"Sometimes. And sometimes it brings the genuinely good things into better focus."

I threw up my hands in disgust. "I don't want to hear anymore. Okay? Don't say another word." I left my house for the last time and started walking over to the Brothers, not really knowing if what Beeflow had said made things better or worse.

But I didn't have any time to think about it. Suddenly from down the street came all these screams and sounds of people running. LOTS of people running. I'd just gotten to Brooks and Zin Zan when this crowd arrived. First came a bunch of men in Roman gladiator uniforms—swords, shields, sandals up to their knees, the whole bit. They came stampeding down the street slap slap slapping on their sandals. Every last one of them looked scared shitless. They all kept looking over their shoulders at what was after them.

When they were gone, a few moments passed and then came the second wave. Maybe a hundred wild- looking, screaming women in leather and animal skins, wearing headdresses made out of crazy-colored bird feathers, carrying spears and swords and all kinds of other ugly weapons, some of their faces covered in war paint, went barreling after those scared gladiators. It was clear that they were going to catch up any minute.

After the last ones passed I said, "What the fuck was that?"

Brooks and Zin Zan started running after them. Brooks said, "Some dead fool chose the movie 'Hercules and the Captive Women' to fill his house. But guess what—they escaped."

"And we're supposed to do something about it? Us? Just the three of us?"

We were already running after them when Zin Zan said, "Now it gets interesting."